Hoons have started treating the roads around the primary school like a racing circuit. A gate is snapped clean off its hinges. The oval is ripped raw by drag racers.

When a school bus is run off the road and an excursion is abandoned, the Serventy Kids decide that it's time to take action.

Can Hayley get the Bumcrack Kid to join the campaign?

Will Sergeant Wilson catch the culprits before Mrs Abernathy slays him with her cakes?

Will Councillor Stott die of embarrassment?

Can the hoons be stopped before someone gets killed?

Anything could happen in this second exciting Serventy Kids adventure — and it probably will!

JON DOUST lives near Perth in Western Australia. His first loves were reading and writing, and he can still do both.

KEN SPILLMAN started school in Sydney, New South Wales, but now lives about an hour's drive from Jon's house.

Jon and Ken meet in the middle, make notes over coffee, and eventually go home to bounce chapters back and forth by email.

MAGWHEEL
MADNESS

JON DOUST
& KEN SPILLMAN

Illustrations by Marion Duke

Fremantle Arts Centre Press

Australia's finest small publisher

First published 2005 by
FREMANTLE ARTS CENTRE PRESS
25 Quarry Street, Fremantle
(PO Box 158, North Fremantle 6159)
Western Australia
www.facp.iinet.net.au

Consultant Editor Wendy Jenkins
Designer Marion Duke
Production Cate Sutherland
Printed by Griffin Press

National Library of Australia
Cataloguing-in-publication data

Doust, Jon.
Magwheel madness.

For primary children aged 8-12.
ISBN 1 920731 76 8.

1. Drag racing - Juvenile fiction. I. Spillman, Ken, 1959- .
II. Title.

A823.3

For all the kids, teachers, librarians and parents
who responded so enthusiastically to our first
Serventy Kids book, Magpie Mischief.
Thanks a million for your emails, letters and
invitations — keep 'em coming!

Hazel,

this book is

yours. Use it wisely.

1

Disturbing the Peace

The Crosswalk Lady held out the orange flags and blew her whistle.

All clear!

Squawky the magpie hopped from one of her shoulders to the other, trying to get a better look at the kids crossing the road towards him. He was looking for Reuben and May because they sometimes brought him insects!

'Hey,' said Reuben, hurrying over the crosswalk with his

sister close behind him. 'We're going on an excursion today — to the Herdsman Lake Wildlife Centre.'

He noticed Squawky eyeing him off, so he added, 'Nothing for ya, Squawky. I've been stressin' out on my snake project.'

The magpie looked at May.

'Come off it, mate,' Reuben said. 'You're not starving. You guys are gettin' spoilt!'

At the other side of the road, Reuben stopped.

'Hey, Bird Lady, did ya hear about Hayley?'

The Crosswalk Lady smiled. Kids called her the Bird Lady because she was a magpie expert, and she had raised Squawky in her own house after he fell out of his nest.

'Nick reckons she's going to get some kind of environment award.'

Nick Robson was Reuben's best friend, and his sister Hayley was one of the school captains. Last term, during nesting season, Hayley had led a big campaign to save the school's magpies from being shot by the local council.

'I reckon all of us should get an awarr ...'

There was a deafening roar.

Tyres squealed.

Rubber burned.

May screamed.

Squawky squawked and flew into a tree.

And a shiny black Holden thundered into Hope Street.

It was hotted-up to the max, with fats on the mags and spoilers all over. It looked like a flattened-out rocket going for the world land speed record.

Its P-plate driver planted his foot. The Bird Lady jumped back and grabbed at Reuben and May.

'Awesome!' yelled Reuben.

'*Not*,' said May.

'Idiot!' said the Bird Lady.

The P-plater hunched low

over the steering wheel as he ripped by, grinning like a chimpanzee.

'Are you children all right?'

The Bird Lady was angry, and May noticed she was shaking.

The Bird Lady had been the traffic warden at Serventy Primary School for as long as anyone could remember, and she'd never seen such reckless driving.

'You go on into school, May, I want to have a word with Reuben.'

She turned to Reuben. 'Awesome? Do you really think so? Idiots like that disturb the peace, and it's dangerous. That boy would be seventeen or eighteen at the most, and he's driving a very powerful car. Who does he think he is, Michael Schumacher?'

Reuben looked at the ground. He'd never heard the Bird Lady talk this way. *Anyway*, he thought, *Schumacher is cool!*

The Bird Lady hadn't finished.

'Cars are fine, Reuben, but speed does kill people, and often. The right place for that car is on the racetrack. If he wants to drive fast, he should get right away from houses and schools.'

'Yeah,' said Reuben. 'S'pose.'

And then he saw his escape. The Robsons' car pulled up on the other side of the road. Hayley and Nick gave him a wave as they hopped out. Two other mates, Marcel and Truong, were walking down the road from the deli run by Truong's parents. They were going on the Year 6 excursion, too, and Reuben couldn't wait. *Excursions are huge!*

2
Skid Marks

The bus was like an oven. The Year 6 class had only just left for the Herdsman Lake Wildlife Centre and already they were sizzling. Truong was sweating like a raw sausage on a barbecue. Nick kept whining about having left his drink bottle at school. He reckoned if he didn't have a drink of water soon, he'd suck Herdsman Lake dry.

'Give it a rest,' Mr Attrill told him. 'Or you can go jump in the lake when we get there.'

Reuben didn't seem to notice the heat

— he was too excited. 'I can't wait to see the dugites! I saw one of them fellas in Grandad's backyard down in Pinjarra. Grandad was gunna chop it, but by the time he found his shovel it'd shot through … That snake coulda killed me with one hit from its fangs. Deadly.' He struck at the air with two fingers bent over like a snake's fangs. 'Deadly! Deadly! Deadly!'

Reuben's mum always said that he had been born talking. She told people that when Reuben was born the doctor smacked his bottom — not to start him breathing, but to make him shut up.

But it hadn't worked. 'I can't wait! I can't wait! Deadly!'

'And *I* can't wait to see the fantastic project you are going to hand in after this excursion,' said Mr Attrill with a wink.

Reuben stopped talking for a moment and groaned.

Up the front of the bus, Tash Abernathy was feeling sleepy. Her eyes kept closing and her clipboard kept sliding off her lap. She unwrapped a banana muffin her mum had made her bring, and started picking at it to keep herself awake.

'Go on, Tash, give us a bit,' said the girl beside her. 'That smells *so-o-o* nice …'

Just as Tash passed the muffin to the girl, the bus driver spun the steering wheel and the bus swerved sharply. The muffin flew out of Tash's hands, bounced off the girl's nose, smashed into the rear-vision mirror and fell on the driver's head.

Tash screamed.

Mr Attrill swore.

Reuben stopped mid-sentence.

Truong yelled, '*What* the …?!'

The bus driver spun the wheel again and hit the brakes. The bus jolted. Tyres screeched. Some kids fell into the aisle. Some slammed into windows. Nick caught a glimpse of a blue Skyline veering out of control and skidding straight for the bus. The bus driver hung onto the wheel and braced himself as the bus hit the kerb. Nick was airborne for a second and landed on Truong with a thump. The bus ran along the footpath, just missing a man with a pram, before lurching to a halt.

'*Madman!*' the bus driver shouted out of the window after the Skyline.

Mr Attrill picked himself up off the floor. 'Is everyone all right?' His voice was wobbly.

Kids untangled themselves and returned to their seats. Outside the window they could see long, black skid marks on the road. Tash Abernathy was making a strange noise — like a wild animal.

'Tash is bawling, Mr Attrill,' said Reuben.

Her arm was hanging at a funny angle. Mr Attrill went to the front of the bus to have a closer look, and then used his mobile phone to call the school's principal, Mrs Johnston.

'We'll have to turn back,' he told the driver. 'Sorry, kids, Tash needs a doctor. We'll go to the wildlife centre some other day.'

Reuben slumped. Nick grumbled. The driver picked bits of muffin out of his hair. Tash had gone white.

The ride back to school was fairly quiet.

'What about those skid marks, eh?' said Reuben.

'I'd seriously kill for a drink,' said Nick.

'I reckon he should be locked up,' said Truong.

'Who? *Nick?* Must've nearly killed ya when he landed on ya.'

Nick snorted. 'I think he means the moron driver.'

Back at school, everyone had to wait on the bus while Mr Attrill sorted things out for Tash.

Year 6 was so desperate to get off the bus, a couple of the biggest kids got jammed in the doorway.

Reuben shoved from behind.

'I need a drink!' yelled Nick.

The bus driver did his best to keep order but was embarrassed when someone said, 'Ooh, yuk! You've got really bad dandruff!'

'It's not dandruff,' he said. 'It's muffin.'

That afternoon no-one wanted to be in class. They were all upset about missing out on their excursion.

'I'm not upset,' said Reuben, 'I'm absolutely *spewin'*.'

No-one could concentrate. It was like the kids' brains had tuned in to different radio and TV stations. One brain was on FM and the next was on AM. Nick Robson was picking up the footy channel on pay TV, while a girl named Holly Bilson seemed to be getting the Home Shopping Network.

'I'd like one of those,' she muttered. 'The free steak knives will come in handy.'

Some kids even seemed to be picking up foreign language broadcasts. Reuben was getting a wildlife show on the Discovery Channel. It was all very strange.

On the way home from school, Nick told Hayley the full story. She stared at him. 'Hang on, Nick, so Mr Attrill told you to jump in the lake, right? Then you flew through the air and landed on Truong, right? What *are* you talking about?'

Truong went to bed early after his mum rubbed goanna oil on his back.

Reuben called his grandfather in Pinjarra. 'Hey, guess what happened today?' he began.

After a while, his grandma came on the phone.

'You can stop talking now, Reuben, Grandad fell asleep fifteen minutes ago.'

3

Gate? What gate?

There were tyre marks everywhere. All over the basketball court, and even in the undercover area. Someone had been burning serious rubber in the schoolyard.

'Doughnuts,' Nick said. 'They've been doing doughies on our court!'

Hayley couldn't believe it. She'd never seen vandalism like this at school. Sure, there had been some graffiti, and Ben Stott and his mates were always hassling magpies during nesting season. And ... oh yes, there was that time someone stuck the garden hose through the high window of the girls' toilets. But nothing like this. The district's revheads were out of control, no doubt about it.

Nick was still looking at the basketball court when Marcel and Truong arrived, followed by Reuben and May. Reuben was talking over his shoulder to the Bird Lady as he came through the gate.

Marcel looked at Nick and saw that something was wrong.

'Hey Nicko, what's going down?'

Nick pointed to the court.

Marcel thought he had it figured. 'Wheelchair basketball?'

'Yeah, *right*. With tyres as fat as a truck? It's the revheads, meat-head.'

Truong thought of the Skyline that had run the school bus off the road, and suddenly felt angry. The bruises he'd got when Nick landed on him had only just gone away. Now some idiot had trashed the basketball court. Who the hell did these guys think they were?

'I suppose there'll have to be a special P & C meeting,' said Truong.

Marcel shook his head. 'No way.'

'You're just scared your dad'll go psycho again,' laughed Reuben.

And Marcel was. It wasn't long ago that his dad had got steamed up at a meeting about magpie swooping and threw a jam scone at Ben Stott's father.

Hayley called them over to the far side of the court. Down on the oval, the grass had been hacked up and there were tyre furrows running all over the place. In a few spots, wheel spins had made ditches. But Hayley was looking hard at something on the far side.

'What are you looking at?' said Nick.

'It's what I'm *not* looking at that's the problem,' said Hayley. 'Where's the gate?'

'Gate? What gate? Didn't know we had one.'

'You wouldn't know if your daks were on fire,' said Marcel. 'In fact, you wouldn't even know if you had daks *on*!'

Then he and Nick started pulling at each other's shorts.

'Today's a daks-free day!'

'Ben can come as he is then,' laughed Truong. Sometimes, they called Ben Stott the 'Bumcrack Kid' because of the way he wore his pants. Even his boxer shorts were slung low.

Hayley was already halfway across the oval, so

the boys tore after her. Marcel took one last dive at Nick's shorts and nearly dakked him.

As they reached the other side, it was easy to see what had happened. The revheads must have got bored doing doughies, and had run some drags on the oval. Someone had spun out of control, rammed the gate and snapped it clean off its hinges.

'Bet it was the same dickhead who ran our bus off the road,' said Reuben.

'This sucks,' said Hayley. 'We've got to find out who these creeps are.'

4

Death by Cake

But Hayley didn't know where to start. The more she thought about it, the more helpless she felt. She was angry about Tash's broken arm, and angry about all that damage to the school. Whenever she tried to think of what to do about those muscle cars churning up the oval and the dipsticks who drove them, she went blank. It was a weird feeling, and she didn't like it. Soon it felt like her brain was being zapped in a microwave.

'If it makes you feel any better,' her mother told her, 'I've heard that Ben

Stott's dad is calling a public meeting. He wants some discussion about youth issues and community safety.'

'Oh,' yawned Nick. 'Whoopee-do.'

Councillor Brian Stott was the president of the Shire of Serventy. He was also president of Serventy Primary School's P & C and Hayley reckoned he was probably itching for another opportunity to big-note himself.

'Mr Stott has rhubarb for brains,' said Nick. 'Knowing him, he'll try to have everyone under the age of eighteen kept off the streets. Permanently.'

Mrs Robson laughed at that — she reckoned it was probably true. Councillor Stott had recently announced that he was standing for parliament — and Mrs Robson was starting to gather support from environmental groups to run against him. Right now, though, she could see that Hayley needed to feel that she was doing something useful.

'Hayley, this is something the police need to deal with. Why don't you go down to the police station and talk to Sergeant Wilson?'

So on Friday after school, while Nick was at cricket training, Hayley pushed open the swing doors of the Serventy police station. The counter wasn't attended so she rang the bell. Sergeant Wilson appeared at the door of his office and smiled broadly as he approached.

'Ah yes,' he said. 'The famous Hayley Robson. You're the girl who made the council see sense over those magpies. I read in the local paper that you're getting an award ... Congratulations!'

'What? Oh, right, the award.' Hayley had nearly forgotten about that.

'Are you okay?' asked Sergeant Wilson. 'What brings you here? You look like you're shaping for a fight — I hope you haven't come in here to have a go at me.'

'I just wanted to talk to you about something. About those idiots digging up the school grounds and causing prangs. I suppose you know that one of my friends had her arm broken?'

'Hmm. Yes. The Abernathy girl. I certainly do know about that. And we *are* making enquiries. A little evidence would be helpful, of course — a numberplate, for example. A detailed description of the driver. That sort of thing.'

'Old Stott has called a meeting — you probably know about that, too. But Mum thinks it's only part of his election campaign. Stott's meetings are useless anyway.'

The sergeant grinned, but decided not to comment. Kids were getting smarter all the time. Smarter and smarter. As he thought about this, he had an idea. It could land him in trouble if he wasn't careful, so he glanced around shiftily and lowered his voice.

'You kids did a great job when you fought the council to save the magpies. Have you thought about ... you know?

'What?'

'Come on, Hayley ... *you* know ...'

The sergeant waved his arms in the air.

He put his collar up. He crept back and forth on tiptoes. He pulled some faces and pretended to hold a magnifying glass. And he winked. Not once, but three times. Wink, wink, wink.

At first, Hayley thought he was having some kind of fit, but finally she realised he was doing a mime.

'Do you mean …?'

'Don't say *anything*, Hayley. I'm not here, you're not here. I've never seen you in my life. Well, maybe once, quite a long time ago. Get my meaning?'

She did. Sergeant Wilson was saying: *Round up your gang of magpie-saving friends*. He was saying: *Be creative. Get the show on the road!*

Hayley felt her confidence return with a rush.

'Sergeant, I'm nominating you for Policeman of the Year!'

Sergeant Wilson always wished he wasn't the blushing type, but he was. Hayley Robson giggled. And at that precise moment, Mrs Abernathy walked in with a plate full of steaming muffins.

'Not *again*,' the sergeant muttered.

Mrs Abernathy beamed. 'Hello, Sergeant Wilson … Hello, Hayley. I hope I'm not interrupting an arrest!'

To show that this was her idea of a joke, Mrs Abernathy held out the plate of muffins. Hayley took one. 'I'll come around and visit Tash tomorrow,' she said, disappearing out the door with her mouth full of muffin.

'Well, Mrs Abernathy,' said the sergeant. 'Let me guess. You've come to ask if we have any news about the crazy blue Skyline that almost hit the bus. Right?'

'Spot on, Sergeant. My Tash is still in

terrible pain. I want the culprit dealt with.'

'And you've come to offer me another tasty bribe? Did you know that's against the law?'

'Don't be silly,' Mrs Abernathy said. 'I just thought you might like something nice for afternoon tea.'

With that, she dumped the muffins on the counter and marched out of the police station. Sergeant Wilson put his face into the rising steam and watched her go.

'I've got to arrest someone before I explode from all these cakes,' he sighed.

The staffroom at the back of the police station looked like a cake stall. Sergeant Wilson placed the fresh muffins on the table alongside lamingtons, a carrot cake, a chocolate cake, a rhubarb and lemon cake, a seed cake, and something else that was supposed to be a cake, but was really a pile of crushed chocolate bars.

5

All Fired Up

Tash Abernathy was counting the signatures on her plaster. She was aiming for a world record. So far, she had 137. The one she liked most read:

Tash broke this arm because she threw it under a girl and saved her life.
Signed: The girl whose life she saved.

Another one read:

I'M STILL PICKING MUFFIN OUT OF MY HAIR.
SIGNED: SERVENTY PRIMARY SCHOOL BUS DRIVER.

She showed this one to May.

They were sitting around after school with Hayley, Nick, Reuben, Marcel and Truong. Ben Stott was sitting on his bike under one of the school's big marris, watching them.

Reuben yelled at him. 'Better get away from there, Stotty ... The maggies might come down and take your head for a nest.'

''Bout time someone used it,' said Truong.

The boys laughed, but Hayley was sick of Ben hanging around to perve. 'So,' she said impatiently, 'what are we going to do about these stupid Mazdas?'

'*Mazdas?*' snorted Reuben. 'That blue one was a Skyline. The black one that nearly took out the Bird Lady was a Commodore. Can't ya tell the difference?'

Reuben's motormouth suddenly

screeched to a halt. Something told him Hayley wasn't in the mood to be made fun of.

He was right. 'Let's get serious, Reuben,' she said, shaking her head so hard that Reuben got dizzy. 'I don't care what type of cars they are. They're driven by losers.'

'They should just go and race around some track,' Reuben told them, remembering what the Bird Lady had said about the pumped-up P-plater. 'Like Schumacher!'

'Fine,' said Hayley. 'But we don't have a track. Unless you count the drag strip that used to be our oval.'

'I know, let's make a bunch of WANTED: DEAD OR ALIVE posters and stick 'em up all over the place!' Truong suggested.

'Yeah, everywhere. Including the shire offices,' said Nick.

'And the library.'

'Mr Arthur's newsagency.'

'Paganini's service station.'

'And every night we'll take turns to hide in those bushes over there and keep watch for the hoons.'

'Now *that's* a good idea,' said Hayley. 'Sergeant Wilson said we need to see a numberplate and write it down for him.'

'And we'll make a banner and stick it up in the marri trees,' joked Marcel, getting a bit carried away.

'Ben Stott's had enough practice climbing, so he could put it up there,' laughed Nick. '*Not!*'

Hayley relaxed a little and smiled. 'Yeah ... *as if!*'

They were all cracking up now — except May. Her brain was just quietly ticking over.

'Ben *would* do it if *you* asked him,

Hayley,' she said. 'Everyone knows he likes you.'

May never said much, but she always made sense. Suddenly, all eyes were on Hayley. Hayley looked for Ben under the trees, but he'd gone. She nodded.

'I'll do it,' said Hayley. 'You guys make the banner. I'll ask him. And tonight, I'm on first watch outside the school. I'll get their numberplates if it takes me all night.'

* * *

Late that night, Truong, Reuben and Nick got to work painting a huge banner made from old bedsheets glued to flywire.

Over on Hope Street, two mighty muscle cars idled near the nature strip. One was a blue Skyline, the other a red Falcon.

'You're history,' crowed the driver of the Falcon. 'This baby's gunna rip your guts out.'

'You're all talk, Simmo. Always have been.'

Tom Simmonds and Spider McNally had been mates for years — ever since Year 1 at Serventy Primary School. Back then, they used to let frogs loose in each other's bags. Twelve years later, the frogs were gone but they were still joshing each other.

Spider flicked a cigarette butt into the nature strip and climbed back into the Skyline. Simmo was all powered up and waiting for the signal.

They stared across at each other, revving their engines. Spider nodded and

they thundered into the night.

In the nature strip, there was a spreading glow around Spider's cigarette butt. Summer was around the corner, and the bush was already dry. Eucalyptus oil in fallen leaves crackled and popped. Flames burst out in the night.

Hayley Robson stepped out from behind a clump of bushes, stuck her pen back in her bag and ran to the nearest house.

'Fire! Fire!' she yelled.

* * *

When the kids arrived for school on Wednesday morning, nothing remained of the nature strip except a few blackened trees with badly singed leaves.

'Those revheads did it,' Nick told the Bird Lady when he arrived at the school's crosswalk. 'But don't worry. We're going after them. Hayley got a numberplate.'

Out went the flags and the Bird Lady blew her whistle.

'Nick, I want you to leave this one to the police. Promise me?'

But Nick had run off.

* * *

Being nice to Ben Stott was a pain for Hayley. It was hard to put all his showing-off and bullying out of her mind, but he was an expert climber so it had to be done. She sat beside him during art, and even helped him glue dried leaves onto his collage. She smiled at him as the bell rang for recess, and caught his eye at lunchtime.

Ben couldn't believe his luck. The best-looking girl in school had finally decided to check him out — and today, of all days, when everyone reckoned she was a hero for calling the fire brigade and saving the Serventy shire from total disaster.

At afternoon recess, Mrs Abernathy arrived at the school. She'd come to pass on some big news — and some freshly baked Anzac biscuits — to Tash and her sister. The constable on duty at the police station had just told her that Sergeant Wilson had taken in the owner of a red Falcon for questioning.

Tash went looking for Hayley and found her telling Reuben about her plan to corner Ben after school.

'Brilliant,' said Hayley, when she heard Tash's news. 'I gave Sergeant Wilson the number of the Falcon that was at last night's fire. I wasn't too sure if I got it down right.'

'They should break *his* arm,' said Tash. 'See how *he* likes it.'

'Sergeant Wilson? Wouldn't hurt a fly.'

'What about a dugite?' joked Reuben, but then he saw that scary look on Hayley's face again and almost bit his own tongue off as he quickly changed the subject. 'So, do we still need the banner?'

'Of course we do,' said Hayley. 'This campaign is not over yet. Catching one revhead means stuff all. It must have taken two or three of them to chew up the oval and burn rubber all over the basketball court.'

'So,' said Tash. 'You're still going to use your charms on the Bumcrack Kid?'

'Go for it, Hayley,' encouraged Reuben.

Hayley groaned.

'Yeah, worst luck. But right now I've got Ben Stott exactly where I want him. You watch. He'll be up that tree faster than your mum can beat an egg.'

Tash didn't doubt it, not for a second.

6

Time to Talk

Ben Stott was down near the bike racks with a couple of mates when Hayley found him after school. Her school captain's badge jiggled as she approached.

'Er, hi Ben ... can we talk?'

Ben played it cool. 'Okay. Talk.' He turned to his mates and whispered, 'Told ya she likes me.'

'Not here. Alone,' Hayley said.

'Woo *hoo!*' jeered Ben's mates. 'Stotty's hot! Woo *hoo hoo hoo hoo!*'

Ben leaned over to unlock his bike and Hayley got an eyeful of bumcrack. She rolled her eyes and looked away.

'Where?' Ben asked.

'The gate. Near the marri trees.'

'Wait for me at the shops,' Ben told his mates.

He rode slowly beside her across the schoolyard, swinging his handlebars this way and that. He breathed deep and puffed out his chest, holding his shoulders wide. Twice in Year 6 he'd asked Hayley to go out with him, and twice she'd said no. Ever since then, he'd waited for her to change her mind. Now it was happening.

'I'll think about it,' he said, all of a sudden. The words just slipped out —

Ben had no idea where they came from.

'You'll think about what?'

'Umm … whatever. I guess when you ask me to go out, I'll think about it.'

Hayley looked at him carefully. 'O-ka-a-ay. Okay. Good.' It was important not to laugh. 'And while you are thinking about it, could you do me a big favour?'

'What?'

Now they were standing under the biggest of the marri trees. 'Well, you know how you're the best climber around here? I want you to show me how good you are.'

'I can climb anything. You name it.'

'Could you get right up to the highest branches of this tree?'

'No worries. Why?'

'I've got a banner. A big sign.' She pointed up at a long branch that reached out over the footpath and part of the road. 'I want it tied at both ends of that branch, and attached to the main trunk so it doesn't flap around.'

'What banner? What's it about?'

'I'll bring it here tonight. Nine o'clock. Will you do it?'

'But won't those stupid magpies go for me?'

'They won't touch you. I guarantee it.'

'Okay. Nine o'clock.'

* * *

Sergeant Wilson was having a heart-to-heart with the young man he'd brought in for questioning.

'Tom Simmonds. You're eighteen, right?'

Simmo shifted uneasily in his seat. Sergeant Wilson offered him one of Mrs Abernathy's Anzac biscuits.

'Relax, son. It's time to talk. I just want to ask a few simple questions.'

'What about?'

'Your red Falcon.'

'What about it?'

'Number plate 1ACI?'

'I dunno.'

'Stands for *I Am a Complete Idiot*.'

Simmo frowned.

'Nice car, son.'

Simmo didn't let his frown go. He knew cops didn't bring you down to the police station just to say nice things about your car.

'So?'

'I used to own a Monaro. Way back, when I was about your age. Down in Collie. Me and my mate used to tear around a track out the back of the golf course. We called my mate "Flipper" because he flipped his ute — twice. Every time he drove into town we'd stir him up. "Hey Flipper," we'd yell, "What are *you* doing driving the right way up?"'

Simmo laughed.

Ah, Sergeant Wilson thought, *I might just get through to this kid.*

'Anyway, the cops got us,' he went on.

'What?'

'Yeah, Tom. They were real buggers in the old days. Took me and Flipper back to the station and gave us a hiding.'

'Hit ya?'

'A few whacks on the back of the head. Taught me a lesson.'

'What lesson was that?'

'If a kid goes wrong, a bloody good hiding is the best thing for him.'

Simmo tensed up again. He shifted his body, ready to run. But Sergeant Wilson was laughing.

'Come on, young fella, I was joking. We

don't do that. And you'd probably sue me anyway!'

Simmo forced a grin. He wasn't too sure about Sergeant Wilson.

'Look, Tom, I've been thinking. What about you and me look around for a bit of land we can run drag races on? We'll make them official. That way, I can take you on in the paddy wagon.'

Simmo's face lit up. He opened his mouth to speak but Sergeant Wilson went on quickly.

'And it'd get you blokes off the streets. Right away from schools, and school buses, and kids who get hurt ...'

That made Simmo squirm in his seat again. He knew Spider hadn't meant to run the school bus off the road. He hoped Sergeant Wilson didn't think he'd been in the Skyline.

'There is, however,' Sergeant Wilson

said, 'the small matter of a fire outside the primary school last night.'

Simmo tried really hard to look puzzled.

Just then, the bell on the front counter gave two sharp trills. The aroma of Mexican cooking wafted into the sergeant's office.

'Right, you better get out of here,' Sergeant Wilson sighed. 'We'll talk more about that fire later. And the drag racing.'

Simmo got up quickly and Sergeant Wilson followed him out. Mrs Abernathy stood at the counter with a plate of chilli buns. She looked at Simmo in astonishment.

'Thomas? *You!* That car! My own nephew! I *told* Denise she was spoiling you … To think that Tash could have been killed …'

'Don't jump to conclusions about that

bus incident, Mrs Abernathy,' said the Sergeant. 'Tom's here on another matter.'

'Oh, my God,' she screamed. 'The fire!'

Sergeant Wilson hustled Simmo to the door before Mrs Abernathy could get near him.

'Scoot, son,' he muttered. 'I'll handle this.'

Then he faced Mrs Abernathy. 'Now, calm down. Young Tom's just been helping with my enquiries.'

Trying to ignore the fact that he hated chilli, he grabbed a lethal bun. 'Wow,' he lied, 'these taste delicious!'

7

Sign of the Times

Ben Stott waited in the dark outside the school, spinning his bike pedal and practising his coolest poses. There was gel in his hair and he'd brushed his teeth. He'd even pulled his pants up — just over his bumcrack.

'Yo, Hayley. You're late.'

It was one minute past nine. Ben shuffled his feet and looked stupid. Hayley ignored him and got down to business. She took off her backpack and got out the banner.

Ben frowned. 'How the hell am I going

to climb the tree carrying that lump?'

'I just wanted to show it to you, Ben. You'll climb the tree with the banner in the backpack.' *Otherwise*, she thought, *you could shove it down your pants and hold it tight with that bum you are so proud of.*

Hayley put the banner back in the bag and held it up so that he could put his arms through the straps. He smirked the smirk that Hayley hated — the one he used when he thought she might go out with him.

'What about the magpies? They don't like me, remember.'

'I've got that covered. Here, put this on.'

She handed him a long blond wig.

'With this on, they'll think you're one of the Abernathys. And I've put some sunflower seeds in the side pocket of the backpack. You never know, Ben, they may get to like you.'

Ben put the wig on. Hayley cackled. Ben blushed. Then he was gone.

Hayley watched him work his way up the marri tree, hand over hand, legs pumping. She had to admire his style. Ben Stott sure knew how to work that butt.

The magpies were getting restless. Squawky dropped to a lower branch to watch the intruder carefully, but Ben kept going. He had almost reached the branch over the footpath when all hell broke loose. It was just like the Melbourne Grand Prix as Spider McNally's Skyline tore into Hope Street, followed closely by a black Holden.

'That car again,' yelled Hayley, jumping for cover.

Headlights and magwheels flashed in the darkness. Ben watched in horror as the Skyline skidded out of control, jumped the kerb, and crushed his bike like a bag of potato chips.

Up above, the boy in the blond wig tried to muffle a most uncool scream. Squawky fluffed up his feathers.

Spider sped on.

Determined to stay calm, Hayley inspected the damage. 'Oh, Ben,' she said. 'It's totally stuffed, and it's *all* my fault. If you weren't being such a *hero* ...'

Ben took a deep breath and kept climbing. The bike had been a beauty, but the feeling he had inside was even better.

* * *

Next morning, the Bird Lady could hardly believe her eyes. Down the road from the crosswalk, in a marri tree near the school gate, there was an enormous sign, splashed on two sheets in blood-red paint. It read:

BIG ENGINES + SMALL BRAINS = DEATH

When Reuben and May arrived at the crosswalk, there was something in May's shy face that made the Bird Lady suspicious. These kids were capable of anything — she'd learnt that long ago. She held out her flags and blew the whistle. On her shoulder, Squawky tilted his head quizzically.

'Please tell me that you *didn't* …'

May always told the Bird Lady the truth. 'No,' she said, 'I did not.'

'Well, thank heavens for that.'

The Bird Lady tried to catch Reuben's eye, but he made sure his eye was busy somewhere else. He was saying precisely nothing!

And when Reuben said nothing, it meant a lot.

* * *

It only took Simmo twenty-four hours to get back to Sergeant Wilson with a

proposal: how about the old, disused trotting track?

'You bloody beauty,' the policeman told him. 'It's perfect. But before we go any further, we've got to talk about your firebug friend. He's crushed an expensive bike belonging to the shire president's son. He's out of control. We know he drives a Skyline. It was him who started that fire, wasn't it?'

Simmo looked away.

'Come on, Simmo, if we don't stop this fella he'll kill someone.'

'He's me mate.'

'Not anymore. He's left you to carry the bag. Did he come forward and own up?'

'No, but he didn't know his cigarette was going to start a fire, did he?'

Simmo suddenly went red. He hadn't meant to let it slip out like that.

Sergeant Wilson winked at him.

'Thanks, Simmo, that's all I needed to know.'

As soon as Simmo left the police station, the sergeant turned to a constable. 'You can bring in young Spider McNally now. We've got enough to start questioning him.'

Then he was on the phone to the owner of the old trotting track and the Serventy Shire Council. That same afternoon, council staff informed the shire president, Brian Stott, of the idea. He was far from impressed.

'Over my dead body!' Councillor Stott shouted down the phone.

'If you insist, but speed humps are dangerous when you're driving fast,' Sergeant Wilson replied. 'Look, Brian, seriously ... This will be strictly supervised — I can guarantee it. And think of the community safety aspect ...'

Brian Stott nearly exploded. 'What about insurance?'

The idea of young hoons getting exactly what they wanted made his whole body feel like a weapon of mass destruction. A police sergeant should know better.

'I swear to you, Wilson, this will never happen. NEVER! Understand?'

* * *

Ben Stott kicked his mangled bike. *Bugger*. Hayley had just rung him — for the first time ever. But after all that effort climbing the tree, crawling along a swaying branch and tying the banner to it, she'd only rung to abuse him.

All because of his dad.

Ruler of the World.

Eraser of Hope.

Stupid, stupid, stupid.

Hayley's mum had heard about Sergeant Wilson's plan. Unfortunately, she'd also heard about Ben's dad's plan to reject it. Without the support of his dad, there was no chance. No chance of organised drags. No chance of Hayley being happy. No chance of ever going out with her. His dad, the Almighty Councillor Stott, had stuffed it all up.

Ben kicked his bike again. He scratched his head, and he scratched his bum.

Then he had an idea.

If there was one thing Ben knew for sure after twelve years and ten months on Planet Earth, it was this: his father hated being embarrassed in public. And he, Benjamin Douglas Stott, was an expert at doing just that.

Ben got to work. Making a sign wasn't hard ... he'd seen the one Truong, Reuben and Nick had made.

When he'd finished, he filled his backpack with biscuits, fruit and his mother's entire stash of chocolate bars. He walked down to school and climbed the tree.

No blond wig.

No fear.

It was awesome. Half a kilo of sunflower seeds, and the magpies stayed right where they were.

So did Ben.

8

All's Well that Ends Well

May was talking quietly to the Bird Lady. Mr Attrill stood with Reuben, Nick, Marcel and Truong. Tash Abernathy had just collected the 153rd signature on her plaster. Hayley Robson was there, too — and *damn*, did she love what she saw!

Two police cars had blocked off Hope Street, and an ambulance was standing by. Groups of kids and parents chatted excitedly. Mrs Robson was handing out leaflets explaining why people should vote for her, and not Councillor Stott, at the election. Three television crews were filming Sergeant Wilson as he looked up into the trees outside the school and spoke into a megaphone. Way up, higher than the kids' huge banner, Ben Stott was perched with a banner of his own:

Suport Sarg Wilsin Or Else!

'Even I can spell better than that,' said Marcel.

Hayley glared at him. 'So what? Have *you* got the guts to climb up there, and sit there by yourself all night? Can't you see he's sending a message to his dad?'

Nick raised his eyebrows. 'I get the feeling Hayley *likes* Ben all of a sudden,' he whispered to Reuben.

'Whatever,' Reuben said. 'But you gotta admit, Ben's totally full of surprises. First he goes up with that banner we made. Then he goes up to bag his dad, and he

67

reckons he's not coming down unless his dad lets Sergeant Wilson run some drags. Them races would be awesome!'

'*Awesome!*' said Nick.

'Are you an echo?'

'Not that … *that!*' Nick pointed to the red Falcon purring at the end of the street. Simmo got out of his hot machine, walked around to the passenger door, and let out Mrs Abernathy. She was steaming, and there wasn't a cake in sight. She marched through the crowd, obviously meaning business. Tash Abernathy ran to her mother to find out where the steam was coming from.

Simmo looked up at Ben. 'Good on ya, mate!'

'Thomas is quite right,' called Mrs Abernathy. 'Good for you, young Ben.' She turned to the crowd and spoke in a shrill voice.

'As some of you know, my nephew is working with Sergeant Wilson to make our streets safer.'

Simmo tried to hide behind the big marri.

'Councillor Brian Stott is standing in the way. I say this to Councillor Stott: Come the election, you won't know what hit you!'

Hayley's mum clapped loudly. She handed out another leaflet and shook a voter's hand.

Councillor Stott caught sight of Mrs Robson as his BMW pulled up next to Simmo's Falcon. Mrs Stott threw open the passenger door and click-clacked down the street in her pointy heels. Her husband followed her, red-faced. Sergeant Wilson hurried to meet them.

'Everything's under control, Mrs Stott. Ben's okay. There's no need to worry.'

'Worry? Why would I worry?' She kept walking and pushed through the crowd. 'Ben's more at home in a tree than in his own bedroom. No, I've just brought him some breakfast.' She put a container of food at the foot of the marri tree.

The sergeant was amazed.

Simmo thought it was a complete crack-up.

Hayley Robson clapped.

May smiled.

Marcel and Truong did a strange jig.

Tash approached the TV crews and held up her plaster cast to them with a pen. She was counting the signatures carefully: 171, 172, 173 …

Nick and Reuben had gone to take a closer look at Simmo's car.

Meanwhile, Councillor Stott's face had

gone from red to beetroot. He rolled his eyes at Sergeant Wilson and held up his hands as if to say, *Women!* Mrs Stott caught him. She faced him coldly.

'Sort this mess out, Brian Stott. Or *you'll* be the one sleeping in trees!' She snatched the car keys from her husband, click-clacked back to the BMW, and drove off, just missing the rear end of Simmo's Falcon.

One thing was certain. Councillor Stott did *not* fancy sleeping in a tree. He studied the ground, wishing it would open up and swallow him. He looked up at Ben. He glanced around and saw Mrs Robson, floating through the crowd like a winner. Her leaflets were everywhere. Suddenly, the future scared him.

He cleared his throat uncertainly. 'Right, listen up everyone!'

No-one listened.

'People of Serventy,' he said. 'Your shire president is speaking.'

Several people laughed.

Someone tooted a car horn.

Ben Stott threw a biscuit at his father but hit Mrs Abernathy.

'I have something important to say,' Councillor Stott continued. 'And it's about the new racetrack.'

Heads turned.

Simmo yelled at the top of his voice. 'Shut up everyone! Let's hear what he has to say.'

'Following visits to surrounding shires, and discussions with interested parties, I have examined the feasibility of ...'

'Speak plain English,' called Mrs Robson.

'... supervised drag racing under the management of the police. It might perhaps be deemed a worthy innovation.'

'I haven't understood a single word you've said,' Mrs Abernathy steamed. 'Are you in favour of the races, or are you not?'

'In short,' continued Councillor Stott, 'given the pervading atmosphere ...'

'Yes or no,' cut in Simmo.

'Yes.'

Reuben ran under the tree and yelled up at Ben: 'Ya've won. Ya little bumcrack beauty!'

Everyone cheered. The Bird Lady looked at May and smiled. 'You kids never cease to amaze me,' she said.

Ben clambered down with his sign, dropping calmly from the lowest limb. A wave of kids picked him up and carried him over to Sergeant Wilson and his father.

'Shake on it,' Ben demanded.

The policeman held out his hand and

Councillor Stott shook it once, glaring angrily at his son.

'Well, Ben,' Sergeant Wilson said, 'I should probably charge you with something. But all's well that ends well. I'm sure your dad would prefer that we forget about all this.'

Then he turned to Simmo.

'You might like to know, young man, that we have charged Spider McNally with dangerous driving and causing malicious damage, following his confession to both crimes.'

'C-confession?' Simmo stuttered.

'McNally gave us a full statement.'

Just then, Tash Abernathy let out an almighty scream.

'Are you all right, young lady?' asked Sergeant Wilson.

'I think I've broken the world record,' Tash replied.

Sergeant Wilson looked puzzled.

The TV crews trained their cameras on Tash, and she held up her plaster cast covered in signatures.

At the foot of the marri, Squawky was making a meal of Ben's breakfast.

* * *

The crowd was gone. Hayley stood alone with Ben, the magpies carolling overhead.

'Tell me one thing, Ben Stott. How come the magpies didn't bother you?'

'Because you said they wouldn't.'

Hayley laughed. 'Yeah, but I never believed that for a minute!'

'You *what*?' Ben blushed. 'Okay, I admit it. I left a trail of sunflower seeds ...' He stopped talking. Hayley wasn't laughing any more. She looked impressed. Ben breathed a little quicker and hitched up his shorts.

'They found the seeds and kind of ate their way up to me. It was way cool, Hayley. One of them even took seeds from my hand.'

Ben blushed again, not because he was showing his new, sensitive side, but because Hayley Robson had put her arm around him.

'Ben, you *are* going to the disco after our Year 7 graduation, aren't you?'

Acknowledgements

Jon and Ken are an awesome team, but they still need the help, advice and encouragement of many. They especially wish to thank Paddy Spillman; Grytsje and Marcel Doust; Tony and Lyn Pitts of Collie; Brian Davis of the Kalamunda Bookshop; Wendy Jenkins of Fremantle Arts Centre Press; Roger Harris of the Herdsman Lake Wildlife Centre; Gina Lowenthall of the Dome cafe at Galleria, Morley; and the Year 5–6 class at Rosalie Primary School in 2004.

What people said about
MAGPIE MISCHIEF

I read Magpie Mischief. *I thought it was soooo good. I told my brother Iain about Ben and how his bumcrack showed all the time. Of course he burst out in laughter. I am now going to read the book to him.* Kirsty

I loved Magpie Mischief. *I felt like I was a part of the book. My favourite part was when the kids moved the crosswalk to the school. It was funny to me.* Kelly

I saw you at school when you read out a little bit of Magwheel Madness, *I was in the class with the boys who wanted bumcrack boy to get run over by a car.* Emily

I loved your book. My Mum is reading it to us again at night so this will be the second time I've read it. Beaudi

*An entertaining story … * Magpie Mischief *is a book for the green at heart, yet it also manages to be fun.*
West Australian

The kids really enjoyed your visit. The two books have proved very popular and are never in the library. I read the book and really enjoyed it. Keep writing!

Dorte Skou, Library Officer, Vasse Primary School

This is a quirky, feel good book. The human characters are true to life, as are the feathered ones. Even the authors are super friendly, displaying their email addresses and promising to write back.

Good Reading guide, The Age

I am so pleased to read this happy, and amusing book which espouses the cause of our black-and-white feathered friends ... The mixture of humour and the message being told makes this a real fun book.

Reading Time

Magpie Mischief *is another in a long list of quality publications from the Fremantle Arts Centre Press, and will provide some entertaining insights for young people with an interest in nature and its interaction with society.*

Strephyn Mappin, www.api-network.com

I liked your magnificent story. I reckon that Magpie Mischief *will be popular in Spring and I will let my teacher read it to my class.* Giovanni

Got something to say?

You can email Jon and Ken at the following addresses:

jondoust@magpiemischief.com

kenspillman@magpiemischief.com

They'll get back to you!